Stunni
Stunts

Written by Samantha Montgomerie

Collins

Stunt artists have a thrilling job!
They screech off in cars and jump
from towers.

They must train hard to act out fights, run at high speeds and jump high.

Stunt artists agree to do stunts so that no one gets hurt.

They start by thinking of the risks.
They train to do stunts.

Stunt artists train to get lots of skills.
Some train to flee in speeding cars.

Some train to slip down flights of stairs.
Some burst out of speeding trains.

Stunt artists act out fighting sprees. They flip, kick and punch in street fights.

8

They train to hurl spears. They train to fight so that no one is hurt.

Stunt artists train to float up high.
They swoop in the air.

A hoist lifts the stunt artist up so they can swoop down.

hoist

harness

Stunt artists train hard for years.
They plan stunts to avoid harm.

They screech, speed and burst on to the screen. They are not afraid to do stunning stunts.

Stunning stunts

Review: After reading

Use your assessment from hearing the children read to choose any GPCs, words or tricky words that need additional practice.

Read 1: Decoding
- Look through the book together. What words can you find with the adjacent consonants "f" "l"? (*flee, flights, flip, float*)

Read 2: Prosody
- Model reading each page with expression to the children.
- After you have read each page, ask the children to have a go at reading with expression.

Read 3: Comprehension
- Look at pages 14 and 15. Use the pictures to recap the book. Discuss what each picture shows.
- For every question ask the children how they know the answer. Ask:
  - Name two stunts in the book. (two of the following: *burst out of a train, flee from a speeding car, jump from a tower or building, motorbike flips, run at high speeds, fight*)
  - Why do stunt artists have to train a lot? (*so they can do the stunts safely and not get hurt*)
  - Do you think being a stunt artist is a dangerous job?
  - Choose your favourite page in the book. Explain why it is your favourite.